New Zealand Shake-Up

New Zealand Shake-Up

Stacy Towle Morgan

Illustrated by Pamela Querin

BETHANY HOUSE PUBLISHERS
MINNEAPOLIS, MINNESOTA 55438

Cover and story illustrations by Pamela Querin

Published by Bethany House Publishers
A Ministry of Bethany Fellowship, Inc.
11300 Hampshire Avenue South
Minneapolis, Minnesota 55438

Printed in the United States of America.

Library of Congress Cataloging-in-Publication Data

Morgan, Stacy Towle.
New Zealand shake-up / by Stacy Towle Morgan.
p. cm. — (Ruby Slippers School ; 6)
Summary: When Hope and her family visit a sheep farm in New Zealand, they witness the birth of baby lambs, experience an earthquake, and meet a Maori shepherd who is a fellow Christian.
ISBN 1-55661-605-8
[1. Christian life—Fiction. 2. New Zealand—Fiction.]
I. Title. II. Series: Morgan, Stacy Towle. Ruby Slippers School ; 6.
PZ7.M82642Ne 1997
[Fic]—dc21 97-4706
CIP
AC

Psalm 23

The Lord is my shepherd, I shall not be in want.
He makes me lie down in green pastures,
    he leads me beside quiet waters,
    he restores my soul.
He guides me in paths of righteousness
    for his name's sake.
Even though I walk through the valley
    of the shadow of death,
    I will fear no evil, for you are with me;
    your rod and your staff, they comfort me.
You prepare a table before me in the presence
    of my enemies.
You anoint my head with oil; my cup overflows.
Surely goodness and love will follow me
    all the days of my life,
    and I will dwell in the house of the Lord forever.

STACY TOWLE MORGAN has been writing ever since she was eight, when she set up a typewriter in the closet of the room she shared with her sister. A graduate of Cedarville College and Western Kentucky University, Stacy has written many feature articles and several books for children. Stacy and her husband, Michael, make their home in Indiana, where she currently spends her days homeschooling their four school-aged children in their own Ruby Slippers School.

Ruby Slippers School

Adventure in the Caribbean

The Belgium Book Mystery

Escape From Egypt

The British Bear Caper

Journey to Japan

New Zealand Shake-Up

9702

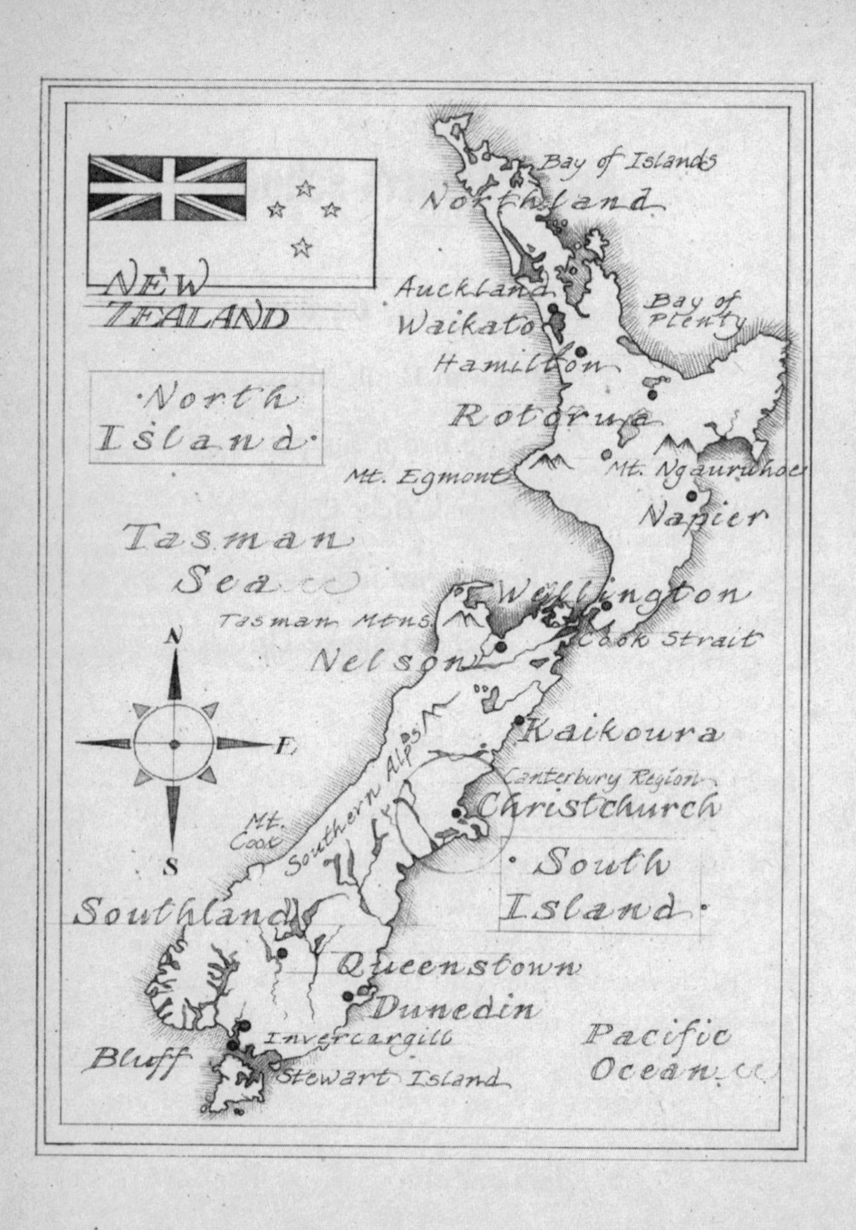

NEW ZEALAND
North Island
Bay of Islands
Northland
Auckland
Waikato
Bay of Plenty
Hamilton
Rotorua
Mt. Egmont
Mt. Ngauruhoe
Napier
Tasman Sea
Wellington
Tasman Mtns.
Cook Strait
Nelson
N
E
S
Kaikoura
Southern Alps
Canterbury Region
Christchurch
Mt. Cook
South Island
Southland
Queenstown
Dunedin
Invercargill
Pacific Ocean
Bluff
Stewart Island

Prologue

Last weekend, Annie and I ran over to Mr. Armstrong's house to return his dog, Max. He had been in our backyard and didn't want to go home.

We dragged Max to Mr. Armstrong, who was cutting his lawn.

"Here come the girls from the Ruby Slippers School," he joked.

He said he'd been so busy he hadn't had time to keep an eye on Max. I told him we'd just gotten back from New Zealand. He ought to see the sheepherding dogs over there. They obeyed right away with just a whistle!

Then Mr. Armstrong started talking about kangaroos and koalas and the "land down under." I guess he didn't know he was talking about Australia, not New Zealand. Even though the two countries are "neighbors," they're over a thousand miles apart.

New Zealanders call themselves "Kiwis" after a

kind of long-beaked bird that can't fly. Can you imagine being a bird and not being able to fly? I love to fly—most of the time.

But that's where my story begins.

Chapter One

"I can't look!"

"C'mon, Hope. You will probably never get another chance like this," Dad said, prying my hand away from my face. "The pilot is flying over Mount Cook just for us."

"Oh, Hope, look! The top is covered with snow." Annie was having no trouble enjoying the view.

I'd like it, too—if we were in a big airplane with lots of other people. I wasn't used to such a tiny plane. I felt like I was sitting on top of a kite. Suddenly, the plane took a big dip.

"Whoa! What was that?" I nearly screamed.

The pilot leaned his head back and shouted, "Sorry, mates! It's a bit windy. I'll be heading back to the station now. Everyone get a last look at Mount Cook?"

I squeezed Mom's hand and rested my forehead on the cold window. The top of the mountain poked up through a thin cloud.

"You know, Hope. That's the highest mountain in New Zealand," Dad said.

"The Cloud Piercer," the pilot added.

A perfect name, I thought.

"You can sit back and relax now, honey," Mom said. She took a comb out of her purse and ran it through my hair. "We'll be landing soon."

The plane took another dip. Mom's open purse landed on the floor, and everything spilled out.

"Not soon enough," I added.

Mom nodded. "I know what you mean."

Dad looked at his watch. "Wow! We've been traveling for nearly twenty-one hours now. It took us eighteen hours to get to Auckland on the North Island. It'll be another three hours by the time we actually land at Dunham Station."

"I just want to get a nice warm bath and go to bed," Mom said, picking up the contents of her purse. "I know it's Tuesday lunchtime here, but my body says it's Monday dinnertime. I feel like I missed a day."

"It's a good thing I don't have to leave again until tomorrow morning," Dad said. "This way, I can help you girls settle in and get some rest before I head back to Christchurch. I think you'll have a great time on the farm stay. Some friends of mine said it was the best vacation they ever took."

Annie sat straight up in her seat. "Daddy! Look at all those sheep!"

I peeked at the green land below. It looked like a vegetable patch. Bushy trees stood like broccoli bunches among clumps of cauliflower sheep.

"They look like cotton balls," Annie said.

"I think they look like golf balls on a putting green," Dad said.

"They're everywhere!"

"You've got that right, young lady," the pilot chimed in. "In New Zealand, there are more sheep than people!"

"I wish I were one of those sheep right now," I said. "I'd like to lie out there in the sun all day doing nothing."

The plane sounded like it was speeding up. "Coming in for a landing!" the pilot yelled.

I held on to my seat with both hands as the plane started to shake and shudder. I didn't feel so great about landing in the middle of a field, even if Dad was sure it was going to be OK.

"We'll be down in a minute, Hope. Just hang on to your hats, girls!" Dad *always* said that.

Before I knew it, we were on the ground. The pilot turned and rested his arm on his seat. "A bit of all right then, mates?"

"Yes, we're fine, thanks," Dad said, ushering us out the door.

He turned back to the pilot. "Thanks again, Rob. We'll see you later in the week?"

"Righty-oh!" he replied. "Let me help you get your bags out of the plane. Here comes Mr. Cooper's farmhand to help you get settled in."

We turned to see a man driving a flatbed truck. It was strange to see the steering wheel on the passenger side of the car.

"Dad, that scared me for a minute. I forgot the driver sits on the right side of the car!"

"It sure takes some getting used to," Dad agreed. "Just ask your mother about the first time I drove a car with the wheel on the right side!"

Mom laughed. "Maybe later. Let's put our things in the car and get going, Reid. At this point, I wouldn't care if the steering wheel were on the roof. I just want to get to the house."

The man in the truck got out and introduced himself. "G'day. My name is Rangi (Rang-ee). Welcome to Dunham Station. Ready to go up to the homestead, are you?"

"More than ready," Dad said.

"Right. Well then, let's just put your bags in, and we'll be off."

He lifted the luggage and placed it in the back of the truck. We all climbed into the back and started off down a road. All around us were green fields and sheep—*lots* of sheep. Every time the truck got anywhere near them, they ran away like a bunch of frightened children.

Several times, Rangi had to stop the truck, get out, and open a gate. After driving through, he got out again and closed the gate. With all the sheep around, I couldn't tell if the gate was keeping them in or out.

As he walked back from opening the third gate, Rangi leaned over the back of the truck and spoke softly. "I suppose you already know that a station means a farm in New Zealand. Dunham Station is one of the larger stations in the Canterbury region. Mr. Cooper has about 60,000 sheep to care for."

I looked at Rangi more closely. His hair was black and curly. His neck and arms were a copper brown color. He sounded like he was from New Zealand, but his skin was a lot darker than I expected.

"Did you enjoy seeing Mount Cook?" he asked.

"Oh yes," Dad replied. "Although we almost couldn't get Hope to look at it. She's a little afraid of heights."

"I understand," Rangi said kindly. "I prefer to keep both feet on the ground myself. My people, the Maoris (Mow-rees), came to New Zealand by boat, not plane."

So he's a Maori, I thought. The Maori had lived in New Zealand before anyone else.

"I see the house!" Annie pointed to a far-off white building.

"Finally," Mom said. "I thought we'd never get there."

"It looks big, Mom," I said. "I hope they have a porch swing. I've always wanted a porch swing."

"I don't imagine you'll have lots of time for that, Hope," Dad said with a smile. "I've told the Coopers that you and Annie are ready to help on the farm. You'll be able to work and learn at the same time."

No matter what Dad said, I couldn't imagine there would be enough to do on a sheep farm to keep both of us busy all day. Was I wrong!

Chapter Two

Two dogs were at our feet sniffing and barking the minute we stepped out of the truck.

"Quiet down, Jip. Jake, is that any way to greet our guests?" Rangi scolded.

When I looked up, several people came out of the house. The screen door banged shut behind each.

A tall man in a white shirt and olive green trousers limped forward. He wore a wide-brimmed hat and held a cane in his right hand. "G'day! Come on in and rest yourselves. I'll bet you're knackered!"

"If you mean tired out, we are," Dad said, shaking his hand.

"You must be the Browns," the man said. "I'm Lachlan Cooper. Let me introduce my wife, Jean, and two of our children—twelve-year-old David and eight-year-old Bronwyn. Our oldest, Ian, is fourteen and is away at boarding school in Christchurch. I'm sorry you won't get to meet him."

Mrs. Cooper smiled and shook our hands. Her handshake was strong.

Dad introduced us to the Coopers.

"It's wonderful to have you here," Mrs. Cooper said. "I hope you'll enjoy your farm stay. We have no other guests right now. We get plenty of rain during the spring, so I hope you're ready for some cloudy weather."

I had to remind myself that seasons are turned around in New Zealand. October is spring, and April is fall. Christmas is during the warmest time of year!

Mr. Cooper tapped his cane on the porch floor. "Let's help you get settled in, eh?"

Before going up the stairs onto the porch, I turned to say thank-you to Rangi for the ride in. He was already walking away, Jip and Jake at his side. His head was down. I wondered if something was wrong.

I asked Bronwyn where Rangi was going.

"Oh, he's headed to his room," she said. She pointed to some white buildings down the road. "He lives down there with some of the other farm workers."

"If you and Annie would like to follow Bronwyn up the stairs, she'll be glad to show you your room,"

Mrs. Cooper said, pointing to the stairs down the hall.

Bronwyn had long, thin brown hair that lay in a loose ponytail down her back. When she walked, it looked like a horse's tail—thin and wispy at the end.

"Here you go, guys," she said. "I put on fresh sheets for you myself this morning. I hope you like the room."

The windows were open, and the cool breeze breathed the white curtains in and out. We put our luggage down on the wood floor. Annie started unpacking right away.

Bronwyn went to the door.

"I need to help Mum with afternoon tea. Shall I call you when it's ready?"

"Thank you," I said.

Annie kept pulling things out of her suitcase so fast they dropped all over the floor.

When Bronwyn left, I shut the door. I felt upset with Annie. Why couldn't she have stopped to say thank-you to Bronwyn? Every time we go somewhere, she starts setting up her stuff the second she walks into a room. I like to take my time.

I stretched out on the bed and listened to the sounds of the farm. What a change from Chicago! I couldn't hear a single car. Instead, I could hear chickens clucking and dogs barking. More than anything, though, I could hear the sheep *baa*ing. Some *baa*s even sounded like crying babies.

"Stop unpacking for a minute, Annie."

"Why?"

"Listen to the lambs. Do you think we might be able to see a baby lamb while we're here?"

"Let's go down and find out!"

Chapter Three

As soon as afternoon tea was over, my family went upstairs and fell asleep until the next morning. We were so tired! The next thing I knew, the roosters were crowing and the dogs were barking.

It wasn't light yet, but someone was cooking downstairs. I could hear the sounds of clattering pans and running water.

I looked down at Ellsworth, my teddy bear, and smoothed down the fur on his nose. "If you were a real bear, you wouldn't be wanted on a sheep station. Bears eat sheep, you know. But all you want is a comfy bed to sit on."

Annie turned over. "Hope, Dad is leaving this morning, isn't he?"

"Yes."

"I wish he didn't have to go. Why can't we go to the city with him? It's going to be boring out here in the country. There's nothing to do."

I thought for a minute. I really wanted to go to the big city of Christchurch, too. "Well, I think Mom wants to stay here. She thinks it would be a great lesson to see how a farm works."

"What's there to see?" Annie said, pouting. "You feed the animals, then they sleep. We're going to be sitting on the front porch doing our school papers all week. We might as well have stayed home so I could play with Susan after school."

"Don't worry, Annie. I'm sure Bronwyn will think of something for us to do."

I heard a car start up, then a knock at the door.

"Yes?"

"Hope, Annie, it's David. Mum asked me to wake you up for breakfast. We'll be eating in about five minutes."

"Thanks." I rushed out of bed to dress. It was cold.

Annie looked out the window. "Great, it's raining. Now we really won't have anything to do today."

Another knock came at the door. It was Dad.

"Morning, girls. Sleep OK?" He gave us each a quick kiss. "I wanted to say good-bye before I leave. I'll be back at the end of the week. That gives you all day today and tomorrow to enjoy the farm before we leave on Friday. Try to be helpful. Keep away from strange places. When I get back, I expect a full report."

"But, Dad, it's boring here!" Annie said.

"Life on a farm is anything but boring." Dad chuckled. "Hurry up and get dressed now. I think Rangi is going to take you around the home paddock this morning."

"Today? But it's raining!" I said with surprise.

"You can't wait for the rain to stop when it comes to farm work, Hope. The Coopers have some extra gumboots and parkas for you. See you downstairs!"

"What are gumboots?" Annie asked.

Dad poked his head around the door as he left. "School's in session!"

Farm work in the rain seemed better than paper work any day. We headed downstairs and met Bronwyn on the way down.

Mrs. Cooper had made us a big breakfast since we'd missed dinner the night before. While we were eating, she explained that Mr. Cooper was using a cane because of a fall he'd taken last week. He had asked Rangi to stay on after the last shearing season to help with the lambing.

"Mr. Cooper expects he'll need lots of help with lambing. That's when the ewes—the mother sheep—have babies."

Annie and I looked at each other. We would get to see some new lambs after all!

"You'll like Rangi. He's quiet but a real hard

worker. Mr. Cooper has asked him to stay for good as our farmhand."

Bronwyn chimed in. "He's good at lots of things, like woodcarving. You should see the things he makes! He loves music, too. He plays the harmonica and the guitar. He's even taught David to play the guitar. We'll have to get him to sing a song for you."

"Where is David?" I asked.

"He's out with Dad in the truck. He's probably working on his dog-calling whistles. Dad's trying to teach David all he can before he has to go to boarding school, too."

"When will that be?"

"He'll go to St. Andrews in Christchurch when he's fourteen, after he finishes Second Form."

"Let's not talk about it." Mrs. Cooper said. "I hate the thought of being away from both of my boys. It's bad enough to be separated from Ian. It ties my stomach all up in knots just thinking about it."

After breakfast, we headed outside with Bronwyn to find David and Rangi. Our rubber gumboots squished in the mud as we pulled our parka hoods close.

"We already have lots of baby lambs. We might even have some new ones this morning," Bronwyn told us.

"I guess you get used to all of this when it happens every day," I said.

"Once in a while, I fall in love with a lamb. Then it's hard to let it go," she said.

The air was still chilly as we walked into the sheep's paddock. The steam rose from the warm bodies of the ewes.

"Aren't they cold?" Annie asked.

"Not with all this wool," Bronwyn said, patting a lamb. "Anyway, it will warm up later."

Rangi stepped up behind me. "If you girls would like to see a new lamb, we have twins right here. They're only a few hours old."

"But they're already standing up!" Annie said.

"They stand up twenty or thirty minutes after they're born."

"May we hold one?" I asked.

"Let's find one that's a little older. David is over here docking the tails of some three-day-olds," Rangi said, walking us to another area.

I could hear the cries of the lambs. "Is he hurting them?" I asked.

David looked up. "Not really. I'm helping them. You see, we put this band around their tails when they're little. Pretty soon, the tails fall off."

Annie put her hands to her mouth. "That's terrible!"

David and Bronwyn smiled. "It helps keep the sheep clean and healthy, Annie."

"But be careful not to step on any tails in the pen!" Bronwyn joked.

David picked up a lamb for Annie to hold.

"You promise its tail won't fall off?" Annie asked.

"We promise." Rangi laughed.

He handed me a lamb, too.

"What are their names?" I asked.

"If we named them all, we'd go bonkers," David said.

"Well, I'm going to name this one Annie, like me," Annie said proudly.

"What are you going to name that one, Hope?" Bronwyn asked.

"I'm not sure," I answered. "I'll have to think about it. Can I tell you later?"

"Good luck finding her again in all these sheep," David said.

I held the lamb close and looked at her white face and pink lips. Her body was covered with tight curls of wool. The dark centers of her eyes weren't round like mine. Instead, each pupil was long and skinny, like a dark rectangle floating in a pink sea.

Just then two men walked by the open barn door. I could smell smoke on their clothes. They leaned against the doorway.

"Looks like just kids and babies in here, mate," one said to the other. He shot a mean glance at Rangi.

"Wonder when the Coopers are going to hire some *grown-ups* to do the job," his partner said.

I looked at Rangi. *Why isn't he saying anything?*

The two men threw their cigarettes on the barn floor and walked away.

Rangi quickly placed his foot over the burning cigarettes to put them out. "The last thing we need is a fire in the barn," he said.

I held the lamb tightly to keep it safe. I hoped everything would be all right, even with those men around.

Chapter Four

We spent all morning around the home paddock, helping to move the sheep where Rangi wanted them. I watched Jip and Jake. The dogs understood all kinds of whistles.

We stopped working at ten o'clock.

"Do you want a cuppa?" Bronwyn asked.

"A cuppa what?" I had no idea what she was talking about.

"A cuppa."

"She means tea," David answered. "This time of day, we stop what we're doing for a cuppa tea and a biscuit."

Just then, Mrs. Cooper came down the hill to the paddock. She was holding a Thermos and a bag of biscuits.

We sat down on leftover bales of wool in the

shearing shed. I couldn't wait to taste the warm tea and shortbread.

The rain had finally stopped. Everything seemed so quiet and peaceful. "I could get used to a mini picnic like this every day," I said to Annie.

Rangi and the two dogs made their way down the road to a row of small buildings. Some men stood beside one of them, smoking. They were not the men I'd seen at the barn.

"Don't mind them," David said. "They're musterers. They move the sheep about. They're not so bad, but I'd stay away from their quarters if I were you. Stay close to the house, and you'll be OK."

"Is Rangi going down to see them?" Annie asked.

"No, he's going to have morning tea," Bronwyn said. "He likes to keep to himself."

As Rangi neared the two men, they yelled at him. I knew by the sound of it that they were teasing him. Jip and Jake barked angrily at the men, but Rangi didn't say a word.

"Rangi should take a lesson from Jip and Jake," David said. "I think if I were him, I'd fight back."

By lunchtime, I was ready to eat again. I felt like I could eat a horse! Instead, I was handed a sandwich of white bread with a black spread in between.

David and Bronwyn started eating right away, but Annie and I just sat and stared.

"Try your sandwich, guys." Bronwyn smiled, black spread all over her teeth.

I lifted the bread and sniffed.

Mrs. Cooper turned around and laughed. "It's called vegemite. It's what most kids here eat for lunch. Would you like something else instead?"

"Yes, please," I said politely. This place was getting stranger by the minute!

Mom handed Annie and me sausage rolls and tomato sauce. David and Bronwyn ate the other two sandwiches, washing them down with chocolate milk.

Mr. Cooper came in as we were finishing our food. He had been out with the sheep all morning. "David, I've got to hand it to you. You're coming along nicely with those whistles. You will make a top-rate musterer if you keep on like this. I ought to have Rangi take you out for a few days so you can help with the dogs."

David didn't say much, but I could tell he was happy.

"How's your schoolwork coming?" Mr. Cooper asked. I thought he was talking to Annie and me, but he was looking at David and Bronwyn. I hadn't even asked what they did for school.

David answered. "I got my scores back in the post yesterday. I'll show them to you when we finish here. Bronwyn should get hers back soon."

So they got their assignments and grades in the mail. I had friends back in Chicago whose parents ran their home-schools that way, too.

"I heard from Ian by post this morning," said Mrs. Cooper. "He says he's doing fine, but one can't be sure. I do worry about him, Lachlan, being in the big city and all. I sent a package to him with Mr. Brown this morning. He promised he'd stop by St. Andrews and give it to him."

"Now, Jean, you're worse than my mother ewes, always looking out for their babies. One up and butted me this morning when I tried to help her little one."

"Did she hit you hard, Lachlan?"

"I'm fine." He held up his cane. "I've got my staff to keep me out of trouble."

"Speaking of trouble," Mrs. Cooper went on, "I want to talk to you about the musterers you have working for us."

Mr. Cooper stood up quickly. "Jean, why don't we take a walk? I've been meaning to ask you about the garden."

He took her by the elbow and started toward the door.

She seemed surprised. "I haven't even cleaned up from lunch yet. Maybe after . . ." Before Mrs. Cooper could finish her sentence, Mr. Cooper had led her out the door.

Mom stood up and started clearing the table. "I wonder what that was about."

"When we were having morning tea, two men stood around smoking and making fun of Rangi. Maybe that's what Mr. Cooper was talking about," I suggested.

David looked up from the table. "I don't think most of the workers like Rangi. They think he's a snob."

"Well, I think they're just jealous because Dad made him farmhand," Bronwyn said. "I wish Dad would get some new workers. Most of them aren't very nice."

Mom sat back down and sipped her drink. "Sounds like they could be a problem. As long as you stay away from them, though, I'm sure they won't bother you."

I hoped Mom was right.

Chapter Five

That afternoon, we headed back to the shearing shed. We passed Mrs. Cooper on our way. She had a basket in her hand.

"Why don't you and Annie go with Bronwyn to gather the eggs? You can stop by to see the lambs first, but don't be too long about it. I need to get on with my baking, and I'll need the eggs to do it," she said.

A few seconds later, she opened the screen door and called, "Girls, I want you to stay away from the men's quarters."

Bronwyn nodded.

"Boy, there's more to do here than I thought," Annie said.

"And this has been a slow day," Bronwyn said as we walked along.

Suddenly, David rushed toward us, waving his hands.

"At least until now," Bronwyn said.

We met him at the bottom of the hill. "Bronwyn, run back up to the house and get some towels. We've run out, and we need something to hold the scent."

She seemed to know what David meant because she ran up the hill toward the house.

"Why don't you two come with me. Another ewe has just had twins."

We headed into the pen while David told us the rest of the story. "The first twin was born, but the mother didn't pay any attention to him. I guess she was working too hard to give birth to the second lamb. Then, before we could stop her, a helper ewe came over and started cleaning off the first twin. Well, once that helper ewe licked the lamb all over, the mother wouldn't take him."

"You mean she's doesn't want her own baby?" I asked.

"Right. He doesn't smell like hers anymore."

"Why can't the helper ewe have the twin for her own?" Annie asked.

"Because she doesn't have any milk for the lamb," David said. "This ewe really needs to stay out of the way when the other ewes are lambing. She thinks all the lambs are hers."

"So what are you going to do now?" I asked.

"Another ewe is about to give birth. If Bronwyn

hurries with the towels, Rangi is going to rub the new lamb with the towel. Then he'll rub the towel onto the abandoned lamb. Sometimes we can trick a mother into taking a lamb that isn't hers."

"I hope it works," Annie said.

We stood back as Bronwyn ran in with the towels. "Here you go."

Just then, one of the ewes pointed her nose in the air and started grunting. "She's been pawing and getting up and down quite a bit. I think she's about ready to give birth," Rangi said.

Sure enough, a bag of pink water came out the back end of the ewe and broke open.

"Oh no!" Annie shouted.

David put his hand over her mouth. "Shhh, keep still. Everything is fine. Just watch."

The ewe walked around for a minute. At last, she lay down and started to push. In a few minutes, we could see two tiny hoofs. A moment later, we saw the lamb's head.

"It's so tiny," I whispered to Annie.

Seconds later, the whole lamb was out. Rangi rubbed it with the towel.

"This helps the new lamb breathe," he said.

David handed Rangi the unwanted newborn lamb, and he rubbed it down with the used towel. He placed both lambs at the ewe's head and watched as she started to clean them.

"All we can do now is hope. Sometimes it works,

and sometimes it doesn't," David said. "Let's leave them alone for now."

"There's Dad. I wonder what he wants," Bronwyn said.

Mr. Cooper was limping toward us. "Hello! How are you all? I've got a job for you, son. I need you and Rangi to head on out to the back paddock and check on something for me. I've heard some rumors that someone's flogging the sheep. I want to make sure the paddock is safe for my Romneys. Some of them will be taken out there this afternoon for grazing. Can you do that for me?"

"Sure, Dad," David said, excited.

"Make sure you take Jip and Jake with you."

"You know Rangi doesn't go anywhere without them."

"Get the four-wheeler and meet me back here before you leave. I need to talk with Rangi right now."

"What does flogging mean?" I asked.

"It means someone's stealing the sheep," Bronwyn explained. "And I have a feeling I know who's doing it."

We followed Mr. Cooper back to the shed. I wanted to find the lamb from this morning so I could finally name her. "I want to call her Lolly," I said to Bronwyn, "after candy." Bronwyn had told me that New Zealanders called any kind of candy *lolly*.

I found Lolly sleeping in the corner of the paddock where we had left her. She was right next to her mother.

"She's stuck right there next to her mum. I guess she's a sticky sort of candy," Bronwyn said with a laugh.

"Oh no! Speaking of Mum, I almost forgot about the eggs. She'll be out of sorts if we don't hurry! Where's the basket?"

Rangi came over and handed us the empty basket. "Forget something?" he said.

"Thank you, Rangi. If there's anything I can do for you, just ask."

"Well, actually, there is. If you are going to the chicken coop, could you walk by my quarters and pick up my staff and my shotgun? Be very careful with the gun. But then, you know how to hold it safely, eh?"

Bronwyn rolled her eyes. "Of course I do. I'll be right back with the eggs and your things," she promised. "C'mon, Hope and Annie."

We headed toward the building where I had seen the men smoking. "Are you sure we should be doing this?" I asked Bronwyn. "You told your mom you would stay away from here."

"Sure," Bronwyn said. "She told us to get the eggs, didn't she? Well, Rangi's room is near to the chicken coop. If you're worried about the musterers, they're not there now. They're off on the back lots."

I was still worried.

We walked behind the building and over to the chicken coop. Bronwyn showed us how to scoot the hens away to gather the eggs. "Just be careful not to break the eggs," she said. "Mum hates it when there's a broken egg in the basket. It leaves a huge mess!"

We worked carefully. I kept looking behind me to make sure no one was coming.

When we were done, Bronwyn took the lead. "Follow me. I'll show you where Rangi sleeps."

I wanted to turn around and go back to the house with the eggs. Bronwyn had promised her mother we wouldn't go to the men's quarters!

We walked into the small wooden shed. It wasn't much bigger than a bedroom. On the table near the door was a worn Bible. I opened it to the page with a ribbon—Psalm 23. *The Lord is my Shepherd. . . .*

All around Rangi's bed were carvings he had made of shepherds and sheep. Some were made from a beautiful yellow wood, and others from a green stone.

"What's this?" I asked.

"Oh, that's greenstone. The Maoris use it to make jewelry."

Bronwyn opened a closet. "His things should be right in his wardrobe," she said.

Just then we heard men's voices.

"Quick!" Bronwyn whispered. "Hide in here."

Inside the closet, we could see nothing. But we heard everything.

There were several men's voices. One of them sounded like one of the men in the barn. "I think it's time we get rid of him," he said.

"Meet us at the back paddock tonight. We'll decide what to do then," another said.

I tried to hold the basket still, but my hands were shaking.

"Look at this," another said. "He's a church boy. Thinks he's so high and mighty, eh? I'd like to shove his face in the mud and show him how low he can go."

I could smell their cigarettes and hear their boots as they left the room. We stayed in the closet long after the voices disappeared.

"I think it's safe now," Bronwyn whispered.

"I knew we shouldn't have come down here," I said. "This is what we get for not listening to your mother."

Annie was almost crying. "I think they're going to do something awful to Rangi. We need to tell him."

Bronwyn seemed to be excited about the adventure. She took charge. "I'll take care of this. Don't either of you say anything to my mum. I'd be in big trouble. This isn't the first time I've been down here when I wasn't supposed to be."

"By now, I'm sure your mum is wondering where her eggs are," I said.

"Don't worry about it," Bronwyn said. "I can handle it."

Just then, David and Rangi stopped by on their motorbikes. "What are you girls doing? You look like you've seen a ghost!"

Bronwyn started to stammer. Suddenly, she didn't seem so in charge. "Well, we . . . we . . . there's . . ."

David shook his head at his sister. "Bronwyn, you know you're not supposed to be here. I have a good mind to tell Mum on you."

"I didn't realize you had a rule about that, Bronwyn," Rangi said. "I wouldn't have asked you to come by here if I had known."

"We don't have time for that now. We need to get out to the paddock before it's too late," David said. "You can tell us all about it later."

They turned their bikes south, and Rangi turned back. "You better carry those eggs home. Your mum's probably wondering where you've been."

What were we going to say?

Chapter Six

"Where in the world have you girls been all this time?" Mrs. Cooper asked when we came through the door. "I couldn't imagine what would take so long."

Mom gave us a hug. "Leave your gumboots by the door, girls. The rain may have left us, but the mud hasn't."

"I was just about to send Mr. Cooper out after you, but he said he thought David would find you."

"Sorry, Mum," Bronwyn said. "Hope wanted to be very careful not to break the eggs, so we took our time."

I bit my lip. *I wish Bronwyn had told the truth. But how do I let her mother know what really happened without saying Bronwyn lied?*

I decided I'd tell my mom later when Bronwyn wasn't around.

"Well, you won't believe what we have here," Mom said, leading us to a corner of the kitchen. "Our very own pet lamb."

Annie squealed.

We knelt down to get a good look at the baby lamb. "It's the twin that was abandoned, isn't it?" I asked.

"That's right, Hope," Mrs. Cooper handed me a baby bottle. "Would you like to feed it?"

I held the warm baby bottle in one hand and helped the baby lamb to its feet with the other.

"Just hold the bottle between your thumb and forefinger. Lay the other three fingers across his nose. That makes him feel closer to you," Mrs. Cooper said.

"So the real mom *wouldn't* have the lamb, the helper ewe *couldn't* have him, and the other mother didn't think he smelled right?" Annie said.

"That's right," Mrs. Cooper said.

"It's been a while since we had one in the house, Mum," Bronwyn said. "Do you think we could really keep it here for a while?"

"Let's see how he does," Mrs. Cooper answered. "I am missing my Ian. Maybe this will make me feel better." She picked up the lamb and cradled him in her arms. "We'll call you Cam, short for Cameron.

"Wait till Ian sees this little one," she went on.

"We'll have to feed him every four to six hours. Any volunteers?"

We all promised to take our turn. "It'll be fun," Annie said.

We heard the screen door open and shut. Mr. Cooper walked in. "I see we have a new member of the Cooper family," he said with a smile. "I suppose this was your idea, Jean?"

"You'll have to blame Rangi for this one," she said. "His only fault is that he's too softhearted. If it were up to him, he'd bottle-feed every one of your 60,000 sheep—and name them, too!"

"I can't see how being a caring shepherd could be a fault." Mr. Cooper thought for a minute. "I'll tell you what, Jean. When Rangi and David get back from their ride, let's have Rangi in for the evening meal. Do you have enough chops?"

I didn't like thinking about lamb chops while petting the baby lamb in the kitchen. I chose not to think about it long. We were having too much fun.

David and Rangi finally returned. After they had cleaned up, we sat down at the table. Before we ate, Rangi said a silent prayer. He seemed to notice we said one, too.

"Well, Rangi, tell us what you found out on the back paddock," Mr. Cooper said, dishing up some potatoes.

"I think David and I discovered some tracks made by an old truck, sir—maybe dog tracks, too.

Looks like the poachers might have been there last night or the night before. Good thing our sheep were in another paddock."

Mr. Cooper looked serious. "I imagine they'll be back again tonight. It might be a good idea to stay out there tonight and keep a watch, eh? Are you up for that, Rangi?"

"Yep."

Bronwyn looked at me, then at Annie. We had to make sure Rangi didn't go back out there.

"Maybe it would be better not to go out there tonight," Bronwyn said. "Some of the ewes are going to lamb tonight. Don't you think you should stay with them?"

"David can do that, Bronwyn," Mr. Cooper said. "Besides, I think I'll ride out tonight with Rangi and stay for a while. It's been a long time since I've sat under the stars like a real shepherd. Don't worry, girls. We'll be back by morning. Everything will be a box of birds."

"If you'll excuse me, I better get ready for the evening's work," Rangi said.

"What a nice man," Mom said. "I can see why you wanted to keep him on. Does he have family nearby?"

"Oh no," Mrs. Cooper said. "He's a loner. Grew up on the North Island in a bad home. He's kind of an orphan, like our little Cam."

"That's too bad," Mom said. "Do you think it's

harder for him because he's Maori?"

"I know the musterers on the farm make fun of him. It might be because Mr. Cooper has given him a better job, or maybe because he's religious."

"What do you mean?"

"Well, he prays at meals and sings songs about Jesus. I've even seen him reading the Bible when I walk down to the chicken coop."

Bronwyn suddenly got up and cleared her place. Annie and I did the same.

"Is it OK if we're excused now?" Bronwyn said. "We are going to go in the living room and play a game."

Now would be a good time to tell Mom about the men, I thought.

"I think I'll join you for a minute," Mr. Cooper said. "I want to sit and read the paper for a bit before I head out."

As we picked up our plates to start back to the kitchen sink, the ground beneath us started to shake. The plates on the table rattled, and the lights flickered. Mrs. Cooper yelled for us to get under a doorway—FAST!

We all ran for a doorway and stood there as plates fell off the table and a lamp came crashing down. We could hear things falling all over the house. Mom held me and Annie so tightly I could hardly breathe.

The earthquake was over in a few seconds. Mr. Cooper walked around to check each room.

I heard footsteps on the front porch. Rangi ran in. "Everyone all right in here?"

"Yes, thank you. I think we're all fine. That was the strongest earthquake I've ever felt," Mr. Cooper said.

"Has anyone checked the lamb?"

We walked carefully through the mess to see if Cam was OK. He stood in the corner of his box, crying.

Rangi picked him up and ran his hand across his back. "It's OK, little lamb. You're fine. Go back to sleep."

I watched Rangi hold the small lamb. He really was a good shepherd. I didn't want anything bad to happen to him. I decided Bronwyn and I should tell him about what we had heard—even if it did mean we would get into trouble.

Chapter Seven

"Turn it up a little," Mrs. Cooper said, wringing her hands. "I want to hear what happened in Christchurch. I hope Ian and Mr. Brown are all right."

"I can't get through on the telephone," Mr. Cooper said. "Nothing seems to be working."

I knew Mom was praying, even though her eyes were open.

"Is there anything on the TV, David?"

"No news yet, Mum."

Mr. Cooper interrupted. "Shhh. They're saying something on the radio."

Just as we'd feared, the city of Christchurch had been hit hard. "They're saying this is the worst earthquake since the Big One that took Hastings years ago," Mr. Cooper said.

"Oh dear. We haven't had an earthquake like this in ages. What are we going to do?" Mrs. Cooper started walking around in circles, crying.

"Jean, there's nothing for us to do except pray they'll be safe. It might not have been so bad in Christchurch as all that. We don't know."

Bronwyn and David sat next to their mother and tried to make her feel better. Mom asked Annie and me to come in the next room with her.

"I want you girls to listen to me," she said. "I know this has all been very scary and you're worried about your dad, but God is taking care of us. We don't need to worry. We need to pray instead."

Just then Rangi came in quietly. "I couldn't help overhearing you, Mrs. Brown. I can tell we have the same Shepherd. I know He's watching over Mr. Brown. May I pray with you?"

"Of course," Mom said.

"Gentle Shepherd," he began. "I pray you will take care of us right now. Please watch over Mr. Brown. I know that you love us and want to keep us safe. Guide us through this hard time. We trust you to do what is right for all of us. Amen."

"Thank you, Rangi," Mom said. "The girls and I appreciate your prayer."

"If you'll excuse me, I must go out and see to the sheep. They are probably frightened, too."

"Be careful. Good night."

When Rangi left the room, Annie snuggled up to

Mom and held her hand. "Mom, isn't it neat how Rangi called Jesus his Shepherd?"

"He certainly knows what it's like to be one," Mom answered. "He's a wonderful example to us of the way God watches over us and cares for us."

This is a good time to tell Mom what happened, I thought. But we were interrupted by Mr. Cooper.

"Gail! Hope and Annie! Come listen to the latest reports. They're saying now that the earthquake wasn't as bad as they first thought. There has been some damage around St. Andrews and the school there, but they haven't said anything about the hotel where Reid is staying."

Mrs. Cooper was still crying. "Oh dear. I knew we shouldn't have sent Ian to boarding school. I had a bad feeling about it all along. And now this! What can we do?"

Mom went to sit on the couch with Mrs. Cooper. "I'm so sorry, Jean. I know how worried you've been about Ian. We can only pray that God will take care of him."

"Yes, but what can we *do*?"

"Jean," Mr. Cooper said, "you must pull yourself together. All we can do is wait. I keep trying the phone, but I can't get through. I'm sure everyone else is trying the same thing."

I sat down to think. With the earthquake, Rangi probably wouldn't be going out to the back paddock tonight.

David seemed to be thinking the same thing. "So, Dad, I guess you're not going to sleep under the stars tonight, eh?"

"It's probably safer out there than in here," Mr. Cooper replied. "But no, I'm afraid everyone is too unsettled to have me gone tonight."

"You're right about that, Lachlan," Mrs. Cooper added. "I wouldn't let you go tonight if your life depended on it. I want everyone to stay close by."

"I think I'd feel better near the phone myself," Mr. Cooper added. "I tell you what, David. Why don't you ask Rangi to bring his guitar and harmonica up to the house. We'll play some music. I'm sure the girls would love to hear a tune or two."

"I'll go make some tea. It'll keep my mind busy," Mrs. Cooper said.

Suddenly, the ground began to shake again. Annie and I flopped down on the couch with Mom. Not again!

Chapter Eight

"I don't know why I ever thought living on a farm would be boring," Annie said when the aftershock was over.

"This probably isn't exactly a normal day on a sheep station," I said.

"You can say that again," Bronwyn chimed in. At the moment, everyone was out of the room but the three of us.

I decided this would be a good time to say something to Bronwyn about the musterers. "Bronwyn, I think we should tell Rangi what happened this afternoon in his room. I wish we'd said something earlier. I don't like keeping secrets like this one."

"We'll tell him when he comes back with his guitar," Bronwyn agreed.

The porch door opened. Rangi and David

walked in. "You wouldn't believe the damage that first earthquake did to Rangi's room," David said. "There was stuff everywhere!"

Mr. Cooper stopped in the middle of picking up a broken plate. "What do you mean?"

Rangi interrupted. "I'm afraid David is making too much of it. There were some things on the floor, and the door was cracked."

"I'm not making too much of anything, Dad," David said. "His door was split in two, his bed was broken up, and the table was cracked into pieces."

"That doesn't sound like the work of an earthquake," Mr. Cooper said. "Rangi, are you sure it was the earthquake?"

Rangi looked down. By then Mrs. Cooper and Mom and the rest of us were standing around him, too. "Well, sir, I believe I may have a few enemies on the station. It could be they saw the earthquake as their chance to do a little damage."

As he spoke, he pulled something from behind his back. It was his Bible, shredded and ripped in two.

"I'm just sorry they got to my Bible before I did."

Mr. Cooper took the Bible in his hands. "I'm sorry, Rangi. I know how much this book means to you. I'll make sure you get another one. Those men are going to pay for everything they've done!"

"Please, Lachlan," Mrs. Cooper said. "Please stay in tonight. There's nothing to be done until daylight anyway. I want both of us to be near the phone just in case Ian calls." She turned to Rangi. "We have an extra bed upstairs, Rangi. Why don't you stay in the house tonight? Mr. Cooper will take care of things in the morning."

"At least they didn't get to my guitar," Rangi said with a smile. "I guess that means you have no choice but to listen to our songs, eh, Hope and Annie?"

"Sing something fun!" Bronwyn said. "David, sing us a verse or two of your gumboots song."

We all laughed as David and Rangi sang.

"Now for something a little more serious," Rangi said.

His voice was soft and kind as he sang about the land of the long white cloud.

"That was one my mother taught me when I was a little boy."

"Tell us a story about when you were little," Annie said.

"I'd rather think about my new life here on the South Island," Rangi said. "I have been very happy here at Dunham Station."

As he talked, Cam woke up and started bleating. "I'll go feed him," I said. "I think it's my turn."

Mrs. Cooper gave me a bottle, and I sat on the floor and watched Cam slop milk all over his face and chin. "You sure can make a mess, just like any other baby."

I heard someone behind me and looked up to see Rangi. "Oh, hi! I didn't know you were there."

"I just came to check on Cam. He looks like he's being well taken care of."

It was quiet for a minute. "I hope Annie didn't sound too nosy a minute ago. She's just curious."

"That's all right. I was just telling everyone how much I feel like a lamb myself sometimes." He patted Cam on the head. "Everyone likes to be loved and fed."

"I know what you mean. It says in the Bible that we're all like sheep," I said.

"I love to read my Bible."

I thought about how the musterers had called Rangi a "church boy."

"What do you do for church way out here?" I asked.

"I go to a house church about thirty miles from here when I can. Most of the time, though, I do the same thing David in the Bible did for church. I worship God among the trees and the pastures. David wrote the Psalms, you know."

"Like Psalm 23?"

"My favorite. How did you know?"

"When Bronwyn and Annie and I went down to the chicken coop to get the eggs, we stopped by your room to pick up your staff and gun. Remember?"

"Yes, I shouldn't have asked you to do that.

What happened anyway? Now that I think back, you looked upset."

"We walked in, and I saw all your beautiful carvings. I especially liked the ones in greenstone. Then I saw your Bible on the table with the ribbon marking Psalm 23. But when we went to the closet to get your things, we heard voices and got scared. We hid in your closet."

"Who was it?"

"We don't know exactly, but they said they were really angry with you and wanted to hurt you. They were planning something at the back paddock. I'm glad you didn't go there tonight. I'm so glad we had a chance to tell you before something awful happened."

Then I remembered what had already happened and felt terrible. "I'm sorry about your Bible and all your things. I guess I should have told you sooner."

"Thank you for telling me now, Hope. I've known for a long time that some of the men here dislike me. I'm sure it will work out all right in the end."

Rangi got up to leave.

"By the way, what's a house church?" I asked.

"Just what it sounds like—a house used for a church on Sundays. A few families meet together every week, and a group leader teaches the lesson."

"Neat. Are there a lot of house churches here?"

"They're all over New Zealand."

I looked down at Cam. He was well fed and fast asleep.

Rangi laughed. “Well, there’s one lamb who has no worries tonight!”

Chapter Nine

I've gotten through!" yelled Mr. Cooper. "Jean, I've gotten through to the boys' dormitory.

"Hello, are you there?" said Mr. Cooper. "Yes, I'd like to speak to Ian Cooper. Yes, I'll hold."

"What did they say? What did they say?"

"Please, Jean. They said that they would have to check. It sounds awfully noisy and busy for one o'clock in the morning."

I looked around the room. Annie and Bronwyn were asleep. I decided to sit down and listen.

"Yes, I see. So you can't really say either way. You haven't got a list, have you? No?"

"A list of what?" Mrs. Cooper was having a hard time waiting for Mr. Cooper to get off the phone.

Finally, he hung up. "They can't tell me anything. They couldn't find Ian. He's not in his room.

They said there has been some damage at the school. Several people have been taken to hospital."

Mrs. Cooper began to sob.

"Jean, you must get some rest and wait until the morning. There's nothing more we can do."

"Can't we drive into Christchurch or something?"

"That would take hours. Anyway, I have no idea how the roads are after the quake. It's best to wait until morning. I'll give Rob a call and take the plane over to see what I can find out."

Mom walked me upstairs for bed and told me to get some sleep. After I got into my pajamas, she sat on the edge of the bed for a long time.

"Mom?"

"Yes, Hope."

"Would you ever send me to boarding school?"

"No, I can't imagine sending you away to school."

"I wonder if I'll ever be ready to go away to school—even a regular school."

"I think you'll know when you're ready, Hope."

"I know I'm not ready now," I said.

"Well, that's good because I'm not sure I'm ready for you to go, either!"

She hugged me tightly. "Good night, Hope."

"Good night, Mom."

I waited until she was at the door.

"Mom?"

"Something else?"

"Yes. I need to tell you the truth about something. Mrs. Cooper told us not to go down to the men's quarters."

"Yes, I know."

"Well, we ended up going down there anyway. Bronwyn said it would be OK."

"You know that was wrong, don't you?"

"Yes. And I felt terrible about it. I shouldn't have followed her. I should have turned around and come back," I said, fighting the tears.

"Many times in our lives, we know what is right, yet we don't do it," Mom said. "I hope someday you will learn to stand your ground and do what is right even when others don't."

"I know, Mom," I said. "I want to be a good Christian. It's just so hard sometimes."

"Jesus didn't say it would be easy, sweetheart," Mom said. "Now, try to get some sleep."

I woke up a lot during the night. I could hear Mrs. Cooper in the kitchen making a bottle for Cam or maybe some tea for herself. Once I heard crying, too, but it could have been Cam. I said a prayer for Dad and held Annie's hand until I fell asleep.

It felt late when I woke up. How could I have slept through the rooster crowing?

I walked downstairs and heard Mr. Cooper on the telephone. "Rob has already gone this morning," he said as he sat down. "Booked a flight at the crack of dawn into Christchurch. I'll have to wait until he gets back."

Mrs. Cooper seemed better this morning. "I don't know how I'll wait. I'll just have to keep myself busy, I guess. Does anyone know where Rangi is this morning? He left awfully early."

"I think he headed out for the back paddock," Mr. Cooper said.

"Did you have a chance to talk to him last night after I went to bed?" I asked.

"No. Why do you ask, Hope?"

"It's a long story, but Bronwyn and I heard the musterers talking about getting back at Rangi. It sounded like they were planning something in the back paddock."

"Those men! They had better leave him alone, or I'll send the police after them. In fact, I think I'll give the police a call and have them meet me out at the back paddock right now!"

"Be careful, Lachlan!" Mrs. Cooper said. "Make sure you take your gun with you."

Just then, I heard a car coming up the gravel road. I opened the screen door and looked out.

Mr. Cooper was standing beside me. "It's our neighbor to the east, Mr. Cunningham. I wonder

what's brought him over this way. Must have lost some sheep."

"G'day, Lachlan!" he yelled out from his vehicle "I've got a package for you and the missus."

By now, Mrs. Cooper was standing on the porch, as well. A young man stepped out of the car, and Mrs. Cooper nearly fainted. "Ian! It's you! My Ian!"

The door on the other side opened, and Dad stepped out. I ran down the porch steps. I grabbed him by the shirt, and he picked me up in his arms. "Dad! It's you—you're OK. We prayed for you. We were worried something awful had happened to you."

"Being away from you three was awful enough."

"C'mon, Dad, we have to go tell Mom and Annie you're here. They're still upstairs."

Dad stopped for a minute to shake Mr. Cooper's hand.

"So you're the one who booked that plane this morning, eh?" Mr. Cooper asked.

"Guilty as charged."

"Speaking of guilty. I almost forgot. I need to get over to the back paddock right away."

"Anything I can do?"

"Hop in Mr. Cunningham's truck, and we'll head out."

"I'll be just a moment. I need to say a quick hello to my wife and daughter first."

A few minutes later, Dad was running down the

porch steps into the neighbor's truck. Ian had already gone ahead with his dad and David.

"Can I come with you?" I asked.

"Sure. I have no idea what we're doing, but hop in."

"I'll explain everything on the way," I said.

By the time I explained the whole story to Dad, he wasn't sure he wanted to have me along. "This sounds dangerous, Hope. What if those men are really serious about hurting Rangi?"

"I had a hunch they were bad blokes," Mr. Cunningham said. "I think they've been poaching in my paddocks as well as the Coopers'."

I told him Mr. Cooper had already called the police. "They're on their way."

"I guess I feel a little better," Dad said. "But your mother won't be too happy with me."

Chapter Ten

How much farther is it?" I asked.

"It's just up over this hill and past that stand of trees." Mr. Cunningham slowed the car to a full stop.

"What is it? Why are you stopping?" Dad asked.

Mr. Cunningham pointed to the top of the hill. "Look over there. See those sheep? They're running away from something."

As he spoke, a huge flock of sheep came running over the hill toward us.

"Stay still and duck down in your seat, Hope!" Dad yelled.

Several gunshots rang out as the sheep poured past our truck. Then it was quiet.

"Stay down, Hope!" Dad turned to Mr. Cunningham. "What do you think happened?"

"I'd say someone got caught," he said.

He started the truck, and we slowly made our way up the hill. Dad wouldn't let me move a muscle.

As we reached the top of the hill, Dad said it was OK for me to look. I could see a couple of police cars and an old truck with blown-out tires. I saw the two musterers being put into the police cars with handcuffs.

As we got closer, I noticed Rangi leaning over something. I wondered if one of the sheep had gotten hurt.

Dad got out of the car. He made me stay inside. In a few minutes, he came back. I saw David and Ian lifting something into the back of the truck.

"What is it, Dad? What happened?"

"It's one of the dogs. He was shot."

I looked around. I could see only Jip. "Was it Jake? Do you know if it was Jake?"

Mr. Cunningham got back into the truck. He shook his head. "Jake was such a good dog. He was Rangi's."

I began to cry. Poor Rangi. He spent a lot of time with Jake. Jake had probably been trying to keep the sheep or Rangi safe when he got shot.

After we got home, Mr. Cooper explained everything.

That afternoon, we sat around the table and listened to everyone's stories. Dad told how he stopped by the school to drop off Ian's package. When he found Ian, he offered to take him out to dinner. It was a good thing, too, because if Ian had stayed at school for dinner, he would probably have been in the old part of the school—the part that had caved in. Instead, he stayed the night at the hotel and flew home with Dad in the morning.

"I knew you wouldn't mind having Ian home for the weekend," Dad said.

Mrs. Cooper beamed. "I have all my family here again. I'm so happy, I can hardly stand it."

"I know the feeling," Mom agreed.

Since Dad had cut short his business trip, he had made plans for us to leave that afternoon for Auckland. We'd fly home the next morning.

"I hope you don't mind, Jean. But I thought it might be best to get the girls home."

"I understand, Reid. I'd do the same if I were you."

"We're just sorry the trip was so exciting. Usually a farm stay doesn't include an earthquake and a shoot-out!" Mr. Cooper joked. "Do come again when things aren't in such a mess!"

"Thank you," Mom said. "We'll miss Cam when we leave. He's a sweetie."

I asked Mrs. Cooper if she would mind if Annie and I went down to gather the eggs before we left.

Mrs. Cooper winked. "As long as you don't take too long."

"Stay on the right path," Mom added knowingly.

"They'll be safe enough now," Mr. Cooper added. "But I think Bronwyn needs to stay here."

I was sorry for Bronwyn. She was grounded for a whole month for breaking her promise.

Annie held the basket, and we walked down the hill past the outbuildings to the chicken coop. I breathed in the smell of grass. We gathered the eggs, then headed around the corner.

"I just want to see if Rangi is in," I said to Annie.

The door was open. I leaned in. "Anyone home?"

No one answered. I looked on the table where the Bible had been. There were two envelopes with our names on them.

"It's as if he knew we were coming," Annie said.

"Open it and see what it is, Annie," I said. She opened hers and pulled out a beautiful piece of carved wood. It looked just like a shepherd's crook.

"Oh, it's beautiful!" I said. "You'll always remember Rangi when you look at it."

"Open yours, too, Hope."

I already knew what it would be.

"It's a lamb," I said, holding the tiny carving of a lamb made from greenstone. I thought of Rangi's hands carefully carving the stone. *I am kind of like that lamb*, I thought. *I need lots of love and care, and*

HOPE

sometimes I follow the wrong people—like Bronwyn—into dangerous places. I vowed right then to follow *only* Jesus. I'd learned my lesson.

"I bet you can put that lamb on your charm bracelet with all your other charms," Annie said. "It'll always remind you of Rangi."

I slipped it into my pocket and started the walk back up the hill. "No, Annie, I think it will always remind me of myself."

The End

NEW

Z-LAND

SHAKE-UP